IN SEARCH OF MY TWIN

Michael Flannery

ISBN 978-1-63630-334-5 (Paperback)
ISBN 978-1-63630-335-2 (Digital)

Covenant Books, Inc.
11661 Hwy 707
Murrells Inlet, SC 29576
www.covenantbooks.com

CONTENTS

INTRODUCTION

This novel is intended to explore the reality of twins, be they identical or fraternal. I have always been fascinated by twins. Part of the reason is that the Book of Genesis reminds us that we are made in the image and likeness of God. "*God created man in his image; in the divine image he created him; male and female he created them*" (Genesis 1:27). This being so, an essential attribute of God is relationship. That is within the Godhead, there is the profound relationship of Father, Son, and Holy Spirit. This relationship is so perfect, that although there are three persons in God, there is only one God.

Since human beings are made in the image and likeness of God, a study of twins and how they interact, can help us to understand better the nature of God. It has been my experience that for the most part, twins have a deep inexplainable bond, not only physical likeness, but also emotional and psychological. However, I will be the first to admit there are no absolutes. The reality is a given set of twins can be very different from each other in every way except for the fact that their DNA is identical, having come from the same ovum. Their genes can vary depending on the influence of environment, nutrition, and the like.

1
CHAPTER

My story is a little unusual. My twin brother and I were born in Memphis, Tennessee, on January 19, 1964. My biological parents were George and Mary Musgrove. They were elated at the birth of my brother, Joseph, and me, (William). Two days after our birth we were on our way home when a tragic accident happened. An eighteen-wheeler ran into my parents' car and they were killed instantly. The car they were driving was turned upside down and there was gasoline all over the place. By God's grace, it did not ignite. Miraculously, my twin brother and I were saved. We had been wrapped so carefully and lovingly by our mother in a bassinet, it saved our lives. The paramedics brought us back to the hospital again to be checked out. There were no broken bones in my brother or me. After keeping us for a day for observation, we were released to the custody of the State Welfare for Tennessee.

Unfortunately, my biological mother was an only child as was my father. Both sets of their parents were deceased and as a result, by brother and I became awards of the State of Tennessee. We were placed in an orphanage in Memphis awaiting adoption. The preference was that we would be adopted together. However, that did not happen. My brother's adoptive parents were from Jackson, Tennessee, and they wanted to adopt only one child. Three months after birth, Joseph was adopted by John and Rachel Adams. John was a mechanical engineer and Rachel a schoolteacher. A week later, I was adopted by Robert and Regina Davenport of Collierville, Tennessee. Robert was a pediatrician and Regina, a nurse.

I must say that I could not have more loving and devoted parents and God had blessed me abundantly. My parents were both Presbyterians and practiced religiously their faith every Sunday. My dad taught Sunday school at Collierville Presbyterian Church and my mother sang in the choir.

I was probably six years of age when my parents informed me that I was adopted. The news that I was adopted did not scare me. I felt very secure and loved by my adoptive parents. We were on vacation in Destin, Florida, when they broke the news to me. They did share with me at the time that I was a twin. I really wondered about my twin brother and wondered where he was and how he was doing. They had shared with me that his name was Joseph Adams. I wanted to meet him and asked if that was possible. My dad told me that when we returned home to Collierville, he would check on it.

My father kept his promise and he called the adoption agency who handled the paperwork. He found out that the records were destroyed in a fire and there was no way of tracing where my twin brother had gone and what had happened to him since then. In the 1960s, there were no computers. My dad did know that originally my brother was adopted by a family named John and Rachel Adams in Jackson, Tennessee. That was all he knew of the adoptive parents and he had no way of tracking where they might be.

The other thing that I requested of my adoptive parents was that they would show me the grave of my biological parents. One Sunday afternoon my parents brought me to Memphis Memorial Gardens. We had no trouble finding the grave. My dad had called ahead of time and was given a map of the cemetery and where the grave was. I stood there silently for a few minutes. There was a picture on the tombstone of both my biological dad and mom. I sat on the grave and examined the picture closely. It was the first time that I had seen them and was fascinated by the picture. I asked my adoptive dad to lead us in a prayer for the repose of their souls. Over the years, I have gone back to that cemetery several times. I make it a point to try to go on the anniversary of their death or as close to that date as possible (January 22, 1964). They had given their lives for my twin brother and me.

My adoptive grandparents were Bernard and Juliana Davenport and they lived in Germantown, Tennessee, just five miles from our home. They doted on me and were regular visitors to my home and played a big role in raising me. They never missed an opportunity to show their love and affection. They made a point to come to all my birthdays, and were present at Christmas, and came to many of my little league games and other memorable events in my youth.

I was educated at Germantown Elementary School, Cross Country Road, Germantown. I went to Collierville Middle School. I graduated from Collierville High School in 1982. As a teenager, I was into all sports. I played little league baseball, soccer, basketball, and I was the defensive back on the football team for my high school. I loved to water ski. My dad had a summer home on Pickwick Lake, near Iuka, Mississippi, and we spent a lot of time there during the summer. I was a healthy child and had only the normal childhood diseases such as colds and flus. I had a girlfriend in high school named Margaret Mueller. We met our junior year. She was an angel. She was a great listener. Margaret was a year behind me. I shared everything with her. I told her that I was adopted and that I had a twin brother somewhere but did not know where he was, nor did I have any information about him. I would love to meet him and to have a relationship with him and I did think about him often and wonder where he was and how he was doing. Every week when I went to church, I would say a prayer for him. I offered a prayer every week that one day we would meet and have a relationship.

I was fascinated by my father who was a dedicated pediatrician. I decided to follow his career and was accepted into the premed program at Vanderbilt University. The only major incident at Vanderbilt was during my junior year, when I came down with appendicitis and had to be operated on November 7, 1985. My parents came to be with me. Everything went fine. I did my MCAT and scored an overall 518 and was accepted into medical school at Vanderbilt. I graduated from medical school and entered the internal pediatric internship at Vanderbilt Pediatric Hospital. The internship was a three-year program with a one-year specialty. I chose spinal meningitis as the specialty and related cerebral diseases.

The summer of my third year of internship in pediatric medicine, I married Margaret Mueller, the love of my life. She had graduated from high school a year behind me and went to University of Mississippi, Oxford, Mississippi, and became a clinical psychologist in 1993. I had one more year of internship at the time. We were wed at Collierville Presbyterian Church on June 12, 1993. Irrespective of the fact that we were at different universities, we spoke on the phone every day. During semester breaks we were together at Collierville. She was the middle child in her family. She had an older and younger brother. For our honeymoon, we spent a week in Cancun, Mexico, and had a wonderful time. I was about to begin my final year in pediatric internal medicine. She would move to Nashville to be with me. She was offered a job at a clinical psychologist practice in Nashville. It had already been decided that I would join my father in his pediatric practice in Memphis upon graduation in pediatrics.

Shortly after joining my father in 1994 in his medical practice in Memphis, I decided that I would hire a private investigator to try to track down my twin, Joseph. At the time, I knew little except for the fact that his adoptive parents were John and Rachel Adams from Jackson, Tennessee. Previously, I had gone online and done a search through missing persons to no avail. All I had was the name. In searching for missing persons, the more information you can feed into the search engine of the computer, the better your chances are of success. I did not know the date of birth of John nor of Rachel Adams. I did not know their social security numbers nor did not have an address except the city of Jackson, Tennessee. The private investigator spoke with eight families with an Adams surname to no avail. None of those families had any relationship with a John Adams. The search proved futile, but at least I felt I had made the effort. I would continue to pray that somehow, someday, I would be successful in my quest and find my twin brother. I could not explain why I wanted so bad to meet this twin brother of mine. There was a connectedness there that I could not explain. There was not a week that passed, that the thought of my brother would enter my mind.

2
CHAPTER

My twin brother Joseph's story was different than mine. When my brother and I eventually met accidentally in 2000, we had a lot of catching up to do. The following story is what he shared with me about his upbringing.

Two months after he was adopted and had moved to Jackson, Tennessee, his father John Adams, was offered a job in Detroit working for General Motors as a mechanical engineer. The family moved to Detroit and that was the reason I was unsuccessful in finding him in my search of the Jackson, Tennessee area some years later. The Adams family had not established roots there.

John Adams was assigned to work in the Plymouth Fury Division of General Motors. Most all cars were big with eight cylinders and gasoline was about twenty-five cents a gallon. John Adams liked his work and advanced with the company to eventually become a division head.

Meanwhile, his mother, Rachel, was a stay-at-home mom until it was time for Joseph to go to grade school. She was a fourth-grade teacher and took a job at the public school system in Detroit. Joseph was enrolled in the same school. Growing up in Detroit was a little different than growing up in the south. In the winter, ice hockey and ice skating were big sports. Joseph loved to ice skate and he was a goalkeeper for his little league team in ice hockey while in grade school.

Joseph's grandparents were Glynn and Rose Adams. They lived in Chicago. Joseph did not see much of them growing up. They would remember his birthday and Christmas. They came to visit only once while Joseph lived in Detroit. Joseph was three at the time and has little recollection of the visit.

A big change came in Joseph's life when he was ten. His father was asked to go to Saltillo, Mexico, where General Motors had a plant in Ramos Arizpe, Coahuila, Mexico. Ramos Arizpe is a suburb of Saltillo, a city of a population of 800,000. This turned out to be a tremendous upheaval in the life of Joseph. He was to go to a foreign country, leave his friends behind in Detroit, and he would have to adapt to a new language, (Spanish) and a new culture.

John Adams brought his family to visit Saltillo and Ramos Arizpe in June 1974. They decided that they would live in the colony of Vista Hermosa (The Beautiful View). Joseph was enrolled in San Felipe (St. Phillip), a bilingual school on Avenida Revolución, Saltillo. John would commute twelve miles each day to Ramos Arizpe. In the meantime, Joseph would have a tutor every day during the summer to learn Spanish and be ready for school in the fall. The Adams family made the move July 1, 1974. Joseph cried all the way on the flight from Detroit to Dallas and then to Monterrey, Mexico. General Motors had a car waiting for the Adams family at the airport in Monterrey to bring them the remaining seventy miles to Saltillo. Joseph was going to miss his friends in Detroit.

Within a week of arriving at their new family home in Vista Hermosa, Joseph had made friends with the children in the neighborhood. At first, they were fascinated with Joseph because he had blond hair. All the neighborhood children had black hair. They wanted to touch Joseph's hair to make sure it was real. Children have a way of communicating with one another and language is not a barrier. The experts tell us that only seven percent of communication is verbal, thirty-eight percent is vocal, and fifty-five percent is visual. One of the first things Joseph learned was the phrase, "mi llamo es José." The next important word he learned the first day was "que" (meaning what). On his second day in Mexico, the neighborhood kids were knocking at his door at 9:00 a.m. asking if he was ready to come out and play. All of Joseph's fears were alleviated having new-found friends.

With the aid of his tutor Maria Garza (a college student), who tutored Joseph for an hour a day, he found he was learning Spanish very quickly. Immediately after his morning lesson, Joseph found he was using the vocabulary he had just learned. He was using it on his new playmates. He also found that the usual soft drinks available in the United States were available also in Mexico. So, he was not deprived of his favorite drinks, which were Pepsi and 7 Up. They were available at every corner store. Instead of dealing with dollars, he had to learn how to trade in pesos. His mother, Rachel, cooked the usual American food at home. However, if Joseph spent overnight with his friends, he was introduced to tortillas and gorditas. That was a new experience for him. In his own home his parents had cable and had access to two English channels on their television. The remaining channels were in Spanish. Joseph found that the summer temperature in Saltillo was not much different from Detroit. In July, Detroit averaged a high of eighty-three degrees and a low of sixty-six degrees. Saltillo averaged a high of eighty-five degrees and a low of sixty-one degrees. Monterrey, Mexico, on the other hand was at least ten degrees hotter because it was about one thousand feet above sea level whereas Saltillo was five thousand feet above sea level. The higher up you go, the lower the temperature gets. It is true to say that the winters in Detroit and Saltillo are very different. You rarely, if ever, see snow or ice in Saltillo. In Detroit, you can expect snow in November and the last snowfall will usually be in mid-April.

Within a week of arriving in Saltillo, the Adams family had found a Methodist church in downtown Saltillo. However, the service was in Spanish. They did find that there were a few Americans in Saltillo. Most of them were mechanical engineers connected with the General Motors Plant or the Ford Motors plant. John Adams' job was to supervise the Mexican engineers working at his plant making engines for Cadillac cars.

School began for Joseph the first week of September. He was a little nervous going there the first day. There were ten children from his neighborhood attending the same school and two of them were in his class in the fourth grade. At the school for lunch break, Joseph was introduced to new kinds of Mexican food such as enchiladas, tamales, frijoles, fajitas, and the like. It did take some time to adjust to the new foods. Again, the students at St. Phillip School were fascinated by his blond hair. Within a week, he had found a host of new friends. Also, there were five American students in the school all connected with either the General Motors Plant or the Ford Motors Plant. There were about twenty American families in all in Saltillo and they formed an enclave. The families shared children's birthdays and adult barbeques together. One of the families had a private swimming pool and that was always a great attraction for the children.

When Joseph was in the fifth grade, he came down with a severe case of acute encephalitis. It was a real scary time for his parents, John and Rachel. Joseph began to run a high fever and was not responsive. His mother, Rachel, rushed him to the Saltillo Hospital Emergency Room and called her husband. The doctor diagnosed him as having acute encephalitis. His father, John, wanted to airlift him to a hospital in the United States.

It so happened that the CEO of General Motors was visiting all the General Motors Plant in the US and Mexico. He included Ramos Arizpe in his tour. He had come by helicopter. Therefore, John had access to a helicopter to airlift his son for medical treatment in the United States. The preferred location was San Antonio, Texas. The attending pediatrician in Saltillo convinced John and Rachel that it would not be a good idea to move the patient. The most important thing was to get the patient stabilized first. It could be catastrophic if the patient encountered difficulties while being transported. The pediatrician was very familiar with acute encephalitis and had access to all the medications needed.

After running the culture, the preferred medication was vancomycin. The sooner he could start the medications the sooner good results would be seen in the patient. It was further exacerbated by the fact that Joseph was having severe respiratory problems and needed to be on a ventilator. The decision was made to stay in the hospital in Saltillo for treatment. Joseph spent ten days in hospital. His parents never left his side.

Shortly after Joseph came home from the hospital, his parents told him he had been adopted. He was very surprised. He had no clue. They told him how both his parents had been killed instantly in an auto accident on January 19, 1964. He and his twin brother (William) survived miraculously. He asked where his twin brother might be. They told him that he had been adopted first and they did not know the whereabouts of the twin. He asked if his parents would conduct a search for his twin brother and they promised him that they would. Again, they assured him of their love for him and that nothing would ever change that love. It was a lot for an eleven-year-old boy to process. They did share with him that his biological parents were George and Mary Musgrove and they were buried in Memphis, Tennessee.

In the aftermath of this newfound knowledge that he was a twin, Joseph began to think and pray a lot about his brother. He wondered where he was and what he was doing and if his twin was aware of him. There is an uncanny bond that twins have together. He decided that he would make every effort to search for his twin when he was able to do so. All he knew was that his name was William. He did not have a surname.

3
CHAPTER

Within the first year in Saltillo, Joseph had mastered the Spanish language. He only had the tutor, Maria Rodriguez, for two months. She was a college student looking for summer work. Once he began attending school, he seemed to catch on very quickly. If he had any questions, he usually asked his classmates. Life went on for Joseph. He graduated from grade school and entered high school. He played little league baseball and his neighborhood had a park in which he played soccer. He became very much a part and parcel of life in Saltillo. In his junior year, he had a girlfriend named Josefina Rangel. They became inseparable. For her fifteenth birthday, he brought her a serenade consisting of a small Mariachi band. Serenades are always brought after midnight. The fifteenth birthday (quince años) is special in Latin American countries. The girl is introduced formally to society. There is usually a liturgical celebration of the event and a huge party afterward. A key moment is when the young lady dances with her father for the first time. According to tradition, she should have permission to date afterward. This does not always follow, depending on the parental permission.

Joseph observed the old Mexican tradition and asked Josefina's father's permission before he began to date her. She accompanied him to his senior prom and likewise he accompanied her to her prom. He shared with her that he was adopted and that he did not know where his adoptive brother was, but that he did pray for him every week and he intended to make every effort to find him when he was in a position to do so. His name was William, but he did not know his surname.

He graduated from high school in 1982. Just after graduation, his father was recalled by General Motors to go back to Detroit. Joseph was happy about returning to Detroit, but he was sad to have to leave Josefina. He promised that he would stay in touch with her through telephone.

Joseph would have to look for a university in the United States. Since his encounter with acute encephalitis some years before, he was attracted to pharmacy. He applied to the University of Michigan College of Pharmacy, Ann Arbor, Michigan, and was accepted to begin in the fall of 1982. It was a requirement that he would have to live on campus in the dorm for the first year. He kept his promise to Josefina and called her every week. In July of 1983, Joseph's father, John, had to return to Saltillo for a four-day conference at the General Motor's Plant. Joseph was more than happy to accompany his father. He would get to visit with Josefina again. He enjoyed the four days and spent most of it with Josefina and their romance blossomed. He promised that he would find a way to bring Josefina on a visit to Detroit in the summer of 1984. She could stay at his home. In the meantime, in 1982, Josefina had been accepted at the Dental School in Saltillo. There were six hundred applicants for acceptance at the Dental School in Saltillo and only 150 openings. However, Josefina did make the cut and was accepted. She was enjoying her study of dentistry. It would be a seven-year program and if all went well her graduation would coincide with Joseph's who would be completing his doctorate program in pharmacy in seven years.

During their college years, the love of Joseph and Josefina grew. There were weekly phone calls and summer visits back and forth. Josefina went to Ann Arbor, Michigan, for Joseph's graduation with a Ph.D. in pharmacy and Joseph went to Saltillo, Mexico, for Josefina's graduation from dental school (Universidad Autónoma de Coahuila, Saltillo, Mexico). They decided to wed that same year and Saltillo was chosen for the wedding on June 24, 1989. Cancun, Mexico was chosen for the place of their honeymoon. It was easier for the Adams family to travel to Mexico for the wedding than it would have been for the Rangel family to travel to Detroit. General Motors loaned their corporate jet to transport the Adams family to Saltillo for the wedding.

Joseph secured employment with the PhRMA, Pharmaceutical Company in Washington, DC. He was to begin on September 4, 1989. Josefina was successful in enrolling in the residency program of Orthodontists in Washington, DC. In the meantime, she was provided a provisional license to practice dentistry under the supervision of the Dental School. At first, Josefina was struggling with the lectures in Orthodontist. While she had studied English for two years as a subject in high school, hearing lectures in technical language was different than conversational English. All this meant was she would have to apply herself more in her studies. The newlyweds settled in Silver Springs, Maryland.

They were excited about beginning their wedded life together. From the beginning of their wedded life, family prayer was always part of their relationship. They alternated back and forth between English and Spanish. Joseph's prayer usually consisted of a reading from Scripture and a sharing of what the passage meant to him. Josefina was Catholic by tradition, but in her prayer, she used the traditions of both faiths to enrich each other. Invariably, Joseph would include a prayer for his twin brother and the hope that they would meet someday. They decided that if God would bless them with having children, they would raise them to be bilingual as Spanish is the second language in the United States. At this point in their relationship they had decided to postpone having children until Josefina would finish her studies in Orthodontic Dentistry. Joseph settled in quickly to his new surroundings doing research for Lilly Pharmaceutical Company.

In the summer of 1990, Joseph and Josefina decided that they would spend a few days in Memphis, Tennessee, and visit the graves of his biological parents. Joseph was amazed to find their picture engraved on the headstone. He had never seen them in person, and it was an emotional moment for him, realizing they had given their lives for him and his twin brother, William. Little did he know that his twin brother was residing in Collierville, a suburb of Memphis. The reunion of the twins would come some years later. Josefina flew on to Mexico to visit her family in Saltillo for two weeks and Joseph returned to work in Washington, DC.

Two days after his return to Washington, DC, Joseph was involved in a car accident where he broke his left leg and was in traction. He, also, had a few cracked ribs, but his injuries were not life-threatening. Josefina insisted on coming back to be with him. That meant she had to cut short her visit with her family. She felt that her place was by her husband's side. After three days he was released from the hospital and Josefina was glad to be able to nurse him back to good health. He would have to wear a cast for six weeks and he would be on crutches. Other than that, he was able to get around and return to work. His work was a desk job and in research.

In June 1992, Josefina finished her studies in Orthodontist Dentistry. Her family came from Saltillo, Mexico, to Washington for the celebration. She joined an Orthodontist practice in Washington, DC. The following year she was pregnant with their first child, a boy, and she named him William after her father. He was born on July 14, 1994. At the time she did not realize that her husband's twin brother was also William. She went on to have two other children whom she named Joseph, who was born on August 6, 1996, and Josephine on September 5, 1998.

In the meantime, I was enjoying my practice of pediatric medicine in Memphis, Tennessee. My wife, Margaret, got pregnant with our first child in 1994. He was a boy, born on June 12, 1995. We named him Joseph after her father. She delivered her next child on June 14, 1997, a girl whom we named Margaret. She was pregnant again in 1999, and delivered our second son, named William. He was born on August 6, 2000. In those intervening years, I continued praying that one day I would get to meet my long-lost twin brother, Joseph.

4
CHAPTER

One day in April 2000, I was reading an article in the Pediatric Infectious Disease Journal, called JAMA Pediatrics. I came across an interesting article about a conference being given in London from June 12 to 16, 2000. It was sponsored by the Lilly Pharmaceutical Company. I had never been to London before, but I always had a desire to visit there. The conference sounded exciting. At first, I was a little hesitant since my wife, Margaret, was expecting in August of that year. She insisted that I would go. I would arrive on June 10th and leave June 19th. That would give me a few days to get over the jet lag and visit a little bit around London. I particularly wanted to visit Westminster Cathedral, I had heard so much about it and the other place I wanted to visit was Canterbury where I could just walk the streets where Chaucer lived. In my undergraduate years, I had been fascinated by The Canterbury Tales written by Geoffrey Chaucer who died in 1400. Now, six hundred years later, I would be visiting there. Another place I wanted to see was the Tower of London.

I made my reservations and I flew Delta Airlines. I had booked into the Waldorf Hilton Hotel, Aldwych, West End, London. Arriving at the hotel, I took a quick nap for two hours to overcome my jet lag. I spent Sunday traveling to Westminster Cathedral and Canterbury. On Monday morning, on my way to breakfast, the concierge at the hotel greeted me by calling me Joseph Adams. I was taken aback and told him that I was not Joseph Adams. He seemed surprised and I asked him why he called me by that name. He mentioned that there was an American guest at the hotel by that name and he was sure it was me as we looked identical. Immediately that got my attention. I approached the front desk and asked if they would call Joseph Adams' number. Joseph answered. I introduced myself and mentioned that I was attending a conference in the hotel. Joseph said he was a research pharmacist and he also was attending the conference. What a coincidence! I asked if we could meet. He said he would be right down.

The minute the elevator door opened, I thought I was looking at myself. It was divine providence at work. He had the same reaction. I introduced myself and told him that he could possibly be my twin brother and we were separated shortly after birth. I shared with him that my birth parents were George and Mary Musgrove and that they had died in an accident with an eighteen-wheeler, while bringing their newborn twins home from the hospital. I had spent my life looking for my twin. What was extraordinary was before I would finish a sentence, he was finishing it for me. We were on the same wavelength. Our stories were the same. We hugged and cried together. How could this be? A search of thirty-six years was over. For us to meet in London, England, of all places—it was God's providence at work. It was our destiny to meet. It was too much of a coincidence.

He was on his own at the conference since his children were very young. I explained that my wife was expecting in August and it was not advisable for her to travel. It goes without saying, for the rest of the conference we were inseparable. It was a tremendous time and we had a lot of catching up to do. We shared breakfast, lunch, and dinner together every day of the conference and talked long into the night. I could not wait to call my wife, Margaret, and tell her. He also called Josefina, his wife, and told her. The two wives were ecstatic and they in turn could not wait to tell the children. We shared e-mail addresses, cell numbers, landlines, mailing addresses, and promised to get together for Thanksgiving. It was decided that Joseph and his family would travel to Collierville, Tennessee, for the Thanksgiving break and stay for the long weekend. They would arrive on Monday of that week and stay the whole week. (Thanksgiving that year fell on November 23rd.)

Every night during that visit to London, I fell to my knees before going to bed to thank God for the extraordinary coincidence of meeting my twin brother. I began to reflect on how our careers were interwoven together. We were both in the medical field. I was a pediatrician and he a research pharmacist. We both had gone to Cancun, Mexico, on our honeymoon. He had three children and my wife was about to give birth to our third child. His first child, William, who was born on July 14, 1994, was named after her father. My name is William. His son, Joseph, was born on August 6, 1996, and Josephine was born on September 5, 1998. It was another coincidence that his first-born son was named William. It was also more than a coincidence that my first-born son was called Joseph, who was born on June 12, 1995, Margaret was born on June 14, 1997, and it had been decided beforehand to call my last son, William, who was born on August 6, 2000. The ages of our children were also closely matched.

On our return to the US, we stayed in touch. Not a day went by that we did not talk on the phone or e-mail each other. With Internet, we shared so many family photos and videos. When the time came to pick them up at the airport in Memphis for Thanksgiving, I could call each child by name, William, Joseph, and Margaret. Joseph also recognized my children and called them by name as did his wife, Josefina.

Thanksgiving 2000 was a memorable time for our family. We cherished every moment together. All the children got along great together. At first, even our own children had difficulty in telling us apart. Which one is our dad? Which one is our uncle? My parents, Robert and Regina Davenport, were very much a part of the festivities. They also were elated. My parents lived in Germantown, just four miles away from my home.

We had planned all kinds of activities for them including a trip to the Memphis Zoo, a visit to the Elvis Presley home, Graceland, a visit to the Peabody Hotel and its marching mallard ducks in the atrium, and finally a visit to Mud Island. There is a beautiful view of the Mississippi River from Mud Island and a scale model of the whole Mississippi River. Incidentally, Elvis Presley was also a twin. His twin brother, Jesse Garon, was still born thirty-five minutes before Elvis at their two-bedroom home in Tupelo, Mississippi.

I took great delight in bringing my twin, Joseph, to my pediatric clinic. The office staff could not tell us apart. That same weekend we went to the Presbyterian Church, Collierville, and the parishioners could not tell us apart. I took great joy at showing my brother around. It was agreed that I would bring my family to Washington to celebrate Christmas there.

Joseph had a beautiful home in Silver Springs, Maryland. His parents lived just a block from his home. They had moved from Detroit to be closer to their son. We spent twelve days at Silver Springs. Joseph brought me by his office and shared with me some of his research projects. I was fascinated that the area of his research in pharmacy was the effects of various medicines on the human brain. Employees at the Research facility were amazed at our likeness.

We toured the following museums with both families together: National Air and Space Museum, National Geographic Museum, National Children's Museum, and the International Spy Museum. We enjoyed the gourmet food at Washington's best restaurants. Both Margaret and Josefina bonded together, and they became like sisters. It was just hard for us to leave and return to Collierville. We took numerous pictures of both families together. It had to be the hand of God working in our lives.

5
CHAPTER

Ever since meeting Joseph for the first time as an adult, a tremendous close bond has developed. I cannot explain the joy I felt in finding my long-lost twin. For thirty-six years the search went on and finally we were united again. We both promised each other we would never lose each other again.

Joseph and I are identical twins. We came from the same ovum. Identical twins do not describe how twins look alike but that they have the same DNA. In the case of identical twins, the fertilized egg splits in two. They are always of the same sex. Fraternal twins on the other hand are the result of two separate fertilized eggs and two separate sperms during the same pregnancy. Boy/girl twins are always fraternal. The genes of identical twins can be different. Lots of factors can affect our genes such as surroundings and nutrition as we develop and grow over time in our minds and bodies. The genetic code can be different making each person unique. The number of twin births is in the low thirties per thousand births. The number of triplet births is one per thousand. Triplets can be identical or fraternal. If they are the same sex, they are identical. Otherwise they are fraternal. Identical twins share the same DNA whereas the third multiple is produced by a different egg/sperm combination and has a unique genetic makeup from the other two.

It is uncanny, but Joseph and I think alike. I cannot say that it is mental telepathy, but I will say that there is a tremendous spiritual-emotional bond between us. There have been several times even in the middle of the day when I will think of Joseph and within a minute the cell phone will ring, and Joseph will be on the other end.

On one of those occasions, Joseph called to say that his son, William, had been playing in the woods nearby his home when he was bitten by a rattlesnake. The rattlesnake was about five feet long. Joseph was not sure whether the venom had penetrated the skin in his ankle, but it looked like it. The skin had been penetrated. I asked him if he had a Sawyer extractor pump as part of his emergency medical kit at home to apply to the bite mark. With luck he had. (A Sawyer extractor is a device that suctions venom from the site of the bite. It is placed over the bite mark and left there for three minutes to suck out the venom and then the pressure is taken off the broken skin site and repeated with the Sawyer extractor). I suggested keeping it in place while transporting him to the emergency room. At the emergency room, they administered the antivenom intravenously and gave William a tetanus booster shot just to be on the safe side. The antivenom neutralizes the toxic effects of the venom. They decided to keep him overnight for observation just in case he experienced any respiratory problems which he did not.

In 2001, I decided to purchase property on Pickwick Lake, near Iuka, Mississippi. I wanted it to be a summer home for my family and I was also thinking it could be a place for my brother, Joseph, and his family to spend some time. My dad already had a summer home there and the lot next to his had become vacant. Growing up, I had lots of great memories of the days we spent at Pickwick Lake. I first learned to waterski there. We went there as a family on lots of weekends.

The site was beautiful and consisted of four acres of land. I built a summer home big enough to accommodate not just my family but Joseph's as well. It had seven bedrooms and a pier for a boat on the waterfront. What I did not know was that Joseph had the same idea. Simultaneously, he was looking at some property on Chesapeake Bay. The property I had chosen was about 140 miles from my home in Collierville and the property he had chosen on Chesapeake Bay was the same distance from Silver Springs, Maryland. The summer homes were similar in size and he also had a pier on the waterfront for a boat. His lot was one acre.

Early one morning in February of 2003, something was telling me that I should call my brother. When I reached him on his cell phone, he told me that he was about to call me. He had just received a call from Josefina to tell him that her mother in Saltillo had a heart attack and it sounded like that they would have to do a triple bypass surgery. The surgery was scheduled for the following day. He and Josefina were going to fly out that day from Washington and would arrive in Monterrey, Mexico, at 2:00 p.m. They would take the bus from the airport, which left every hour, and go to Saltillo and get a taxi from the bus terminal to the hospital. It was most unusual for me to call early in the morning as we usually communicated in the afternoon or evening. I cannot explain why I was prompted to call that morning. The surgery on Joseph's mother-in-law was successful, and she returned home from the hospital after seven days.

The psychic communication was the same for Joseph. My wife, Margaret, had a car accident in October of 2004. I was on my way to the hospital to do my rounds. My wife had just dropped off the children at school, when a car ran the red light and ploughed into her. I had just received the call about the accident when Joseph called to ask if everything was okay. I told him about the accident that Margaret had. She was being transported to the emergency room and her car was totaled. I was on my way there. Joseph could not explain why he wanted to call me that morning. We both remarked that it was uncanny for something like this to happen. Could it be that identical twins have an unexplained power of communicating with one another?

In October 2005, I had just finished my hospital rounds when out of the blue, I felt the urge to call my brother, Joseph. He was just about to call me too. It seems that his oldest son, William's, nose was secreting blood and puss. William could only breathe through his mouth. His face was swollen. Joseph was about to bring him to the emergency room. I told him that it could possibly be Juvenile Angiofibroma. A tumor had formed in his nasal passage caused by an overgrowth of dilated blood vessels in the nasal passage. He would need to see an Ear, Nose, and Throat Specialist. With modern techniques today, the surgery is not very complicated. However, it did need immediate attention. Again, it was an example of the extraordinary way my twin and I could sense a danger approaching and communicate with each other. There have been other instances since we met in 2000 that this has happened. The ones quoted above are examples of what I can recall.

None of our children seemed to have the same power of communicating as I have with my twin brother. All the children related well to each other, and were great friends, and communicated nearly daily with each other when apart, but the telepathic communication was not there. Maybe it is not fair to call it telepathic, but it is unexplainable and there were too many incidents of that sensation.

The close bond that I feel I have with my twin brother has been a great blessing to me. We could not be closer than we are. It has helped us to blend our families together and to have a tremendous bond between our respective children. It was great to see the children deepening the relationship with each visit back and forth that we would make. I would take two weeks off every summer, and a week at Christmas time, and a few days at Thanksgiving. Joseph would coincide his vacation time the same way and that gave us quality time together.

I do not claim that all identical twins think alike or have the same emotions. Even identical twins can be very dissimilar to each other. This is particularly true when they come to their teenage years. It is true that parents tend to dress twins alike. However, there comes a time when the twins want to assert their individual personality. Identical twins with identical DNA may have different genes activate differently causing the twins to look differently, act differently, and even develop different diseases such as cancer. It is not usual for twins to die from the same disease. Twins can have very different personalities. One could tend to be outgoing and the other shy. Twins can also drift apart from one another as they grow older. A lot of factors, such as environment and the food we eat, can affect the way we grow and develop. Different experiences can affect the brain and how we respond to situations we find ourselves in. As a result, identical and fraternal twins can be very different from each other. There are no absolutes when it comes to twins, either identical or fraternal.

6
CHAPTER

In 2002, I heard of a town in Ohio called Twinsburg. Every year since 1976, the town sponsors the largest world gathering of identical, fraternal, triplets, and quads or any other combination. It is a three-day festival. The history of the town is interesting. In the early nineteenth century, identical twins made a proposal to the town fathers. At the time the town was called Millsville. The proposal contained an offer of four thousand acres of land to build a public square and $20 to build a school. In return the town would have to be named Twinsburg and a school to be built there. From that humble beginning, a tradition arose over time to have a festival honoring twins or combinations thereof.

I will admit that people who are attracted to this festival want to give expression to the reality that they are twins and that means something special to them. People come from all over for this three-day festival, usually held early August every year. I have met people from Canada, the US, South America, Europe, and Australia. There is great food, music, lots of activities and sports for children to entertain themselves. The tickets for the festival are moderately priced. It is my understanding that if you are a resident of Twinsburg there is no entry fee.

Participants come in all shapes and sizes. They make every effort to dress alike. It is mind boggling to just walk down any street in the town where you see so many twins in one place. The stories that people share with one another could fill a library.

Joseph and I decided that we would go for the festival in August of 2002. Our families would come with us for the experience. We flew to Akron, Ohio, and rented cars for the twenty-five-mile journey to Twinsburg. Joseph's family and mine were booked at the Hilton Garden Inn, Twinsburg/Cleveland. We had made the booking six months in advance because hotels in the area fill up quickly for the festival.

It was such a great experience that we have returned to Twinsburg nearly every year since. What is most astonishing is watching the awe in the faces of our children as they come to meet other children who are identical or fraternal twins, triplets, or quads. Twins make a special effort to dress alike. For the days of the festival it looks like half the world is made up of twins or triplets.

Over time we have established relationships with identical twins in different parts of the US that we first met in Twinsburg. There are the Harrison identical twins, Michael and James Harrison, from Boston, Massachusetts. Both are attorneys and work for the same law firm. From kindergarten, they have gone to the same schools and also for undergraduate and law school. Both are plaintiff lawyers and represent clients in a variety of cases. Then, there are the Kingston identical twins, Mary and Jane. Both had never left each other's side since birth. They were from Seattle, Washington. They were now in their early twenties and had just graduated from college as teachers. They had secured positions in the same grade school in Seattle. Both were teaching the fourth grade. There are the McCullough twins, Brenden and Donald. They were engineers and worked for Ford Motor Company in Detroit, Michigan. One was a mechanical engineer and the other an electrical engineer. Both were in their fifties. Their wives and children were also with them. Also there were the Bruno twins from Montgomery, Alabama. Their names were Alfred and Allen. They were certified accountants and worked for the same accounting firm. They were in their early sixties. They married the same year and two years later bought homes adjacent to one another. They raised their families together and belonged to the same Methodist church. Their children were now grown and had lives of their own. Having their homes adjacent to one another made a tremendous bond between their children.

An interesting set of identical twins were called Catherine and Celeste Johnson from New Orleans, Louisiana. When we first met them in 2003 in Twinsburg, Ohio, they had just graduated from East Jefferson High School in Metairie, Louisiana. For a graduation present their parents decided to bring them to Twinsburg. Both were enrolled in LSU, Baton Rouge, Louisiana and both intended to study dentistry. They did everything together always. At times, they would swap boyfriends and the boyfriend would not even know that he was with the twin sister.

The common denominator running through all these experiences was the tremendous bond that existed between twins…be they identical or fraternal. It was a psychological and emotional bond. Reflecting on that reality led me back to reflect on the nature of God. When we look at God as portrayed in the Bible, we find that the inner nature of God is relationship. Within the Godhead, there is Father, Son, and Holy Spirit. Yet there is only one God.

In the Old Testament, God revealed himself gradually. The Jewish people understood God to be monotheistic, that is there is only one God. When Jesus came on the scene and began to reveal himself, he did this in a Jewish way. So many places in the gospels where we find Jesus instructing people to keep quiet about who he was. It is called "The Messianic Secret." In many of the miracles he performed, his instruction was to "tell nobody."

At the beginning of his public ministry, he did not come out and say that he was God. The revelation was gradual. He used messianic terms to describe himself. He called himself "the Son of David" or the "Son of Man."

In Matthew's gospel, he traces the genealogy of Jesus back to Abraham. He has three sets of generations each with fourteen generations. In Hebrew, gematria (numeral value) fourteen means David. Matthew introduces Jesus very definitely as the Son of David. The preferred title that Jesus used to describe himself was "The Son of Man." While no one ever called him "the Son of Man," Jesus himself did call himself by that title. We find it eighty-two times in the gospels. Matthew mentions it thirty-two times, Mark has it fourteen times, Luke, twenty-six, and John ten times.

The Son of Man, messianic term, comes from the Book of Daniel. The term emphasizes both the humanity and divinity of the Son of Man. Chapter seven of the book begins with a vision where four beasts are portrayed. These beasts represented four kingdoms who reigned over the Israelites, namely the Babylonians, Persians, the Greeks, and the Romans. The Son of Man was to come during the occupation of the Romans. While he was in human form, he was also divine. Jesus was the fulfillment of that prophecy.

> *As the visions during the night continued, I saw one like a son of man coming on the clouds of heaven; When he reached the Ancient One and was presented before him, He received dominion, glory, and kingship; nations and peoples of every language serve him. His dominion is an everlasting dominion and that shall not be taken away and his kingship shall not be destroyed.* (Daniel 7:13–14)

During his trial before the Sanhedrin, in the three synoptic gospels, Jesus openly acknowledged that he was indeed the Son of Man and went on to claim his divinity since he would accompany his Father sitting on the throne of God.

> *The high priest then said to him: "I order you to tell us under oath whether you are the Messiah, the Son of God." Jesus answered: "It is you who say it. But I tell you this: Soon you will see the Son of Man seated at the right hand of the power and coming on the clouds of heaven." At this the high priest tore his robes: "He has blasphemed! What further need do we have of witnesses?"* (Matt 26:63–66).

> *Once again, the high priest interrogated him: "Are you the Messiah, the Son of the Blessed One?" Then Jesus answered: "I am; and you will see the Son of Man seated at the right hand of the Power*

and coming with the clouds of heaven." At this the high priest tore his robes and said: "What further need do we have of witnesses?" (Mark 14:61–64)

At daybreak, the elders of the people, the chief priests, and the scribes assembled again. Once they had brought him before the council, they said, "Tell us, are you the Messiah?" He replied, "If I tell you, you will not believe me, and if I question you, you will not answer. This much only will I say, 'From now on, the Son of Man will have his seat at the right hand of the Power of God'" So you are the Son of God?" they asked in chorus. He answered, "It is you who say that I am." They said, "What further need do we have of witnesses? We have heard it from his own mouth." (Luke 22:66–71)

There is no question that the Sanhedrin understood the claim of Jesus to be divine because they accused him of blasphemy.

In John, Jesus claims equality with God his Father.

The Father and I are one. (John 10:30).

During his last discourse with his apostles on the night of the Passover, he promised to send the Holy Spirit.

I will ask the Father and he will send you another Paraclete—to be with you always: the Spirit of truth, whom the world cannot accept, since it neither sees him nor recognizes him; but you can recognize him because he remains in you and will be within you. (John 14:16–17)

If I fail to go, the Paraclete will never come to you, whereas if I go, I will send him to you. When he comes, he will prove the world wrong about sin, about justice, about condemnation. About sin—in that they refuse to believe in me; about justice— from the fact that I go to the Father and you will see me no more; about condemnation—for the prince of this world is already condemned." (John 16:7–11)

In Luke's writings, he takes the position that the Old Testament was the time of the Father, the New Testament is the time of the Son, and the period after Pentecost is the time of the Holy Spirit. We now live in the time of the Holy Spirit.

All of this makes me reflect on the fact that within the Godhead, there is Father, Son, and Holy Spirit. That relationship is so profound, so intimate, and held together with an infinite love that there is only one God. By analogy, in a small way, twins, whether identical or fraternal, reflect the nature of God because of the closeness of the bond between them. The same can be said for marriage as it was intended by God. The love of the husband for his wife and the love of the wife for her husband are so profound, they come together and are one in mind, and heart, and spirit. There is no other relationship or bond in this world that is quite like it by comparison. People form different kinds of relationships, agreements, and bonds. There are fraternities, sororities, covenants, agreements, contracts, but none of these can compare to marriage.

In John's first letter, there is a beautiful hymn describing the nature of God as love.

Beloved, let us love one another because love is of God; everyone who loves is begotten of God and has knowledge of God. The man without love knows nothing of God because God is love. God's love was revealed in this way: he sent his only Son to the world that we might have life through him. Love then consists in this: not that we have loved God but that he has loved us and has sent his Son as an offering for our sins. Beloved if God has loved us so, we must have the same love for one another. No one has ever seen God. Yet if we love one another God dwells in us, and his love is brought to perfection in us. The way we know we remain in him and he in us is that he has given us his Spirit. We have seen for ourselves and can testify, that the Father sent the Son as savior of the world. When anyone acknowledges that Jesus is the Son of God, God dwells in him and he in God. We have come to acknowledge and believe in the love that God has for us. God is love and he who abides in love abides in God and God in him. (1 John 4:7–16)

We can conclude from this that any experience of love is an experience of God because God is love. God in his goodness manifests himself to us in many beautiful ways. We need to sensitize ourselves to the presence of God working in our lives and manifesting himself to us.

I thank God daily for the gift of finding my lost twin brother, Joseph. I have made every effort to make up for those lost thirty-six years while we were apart. That bond between us continues to grow and deepen. I salute twins everywhere, whether they be identical or fraternal. I identify with them because of the close bond that God has blessed us in allowing us to be born as twins.

CONCLUSION

I began this novel by stating that there are no absolutes when it comes to the study of twins. However, the presumption is that if God blesses a person by making him or her a twin, a close study will find a deep and lasting bond which joins them together. It is not only their identical looks or features (at times they will not always be identical), but reaches into the emotional and spiritual realm.

I hope that you have enjoyed reading this book as much as I have enjoyed writing it. It is my contention that twins reflect in a small way the inner nature of the Godhead. Within God, there are three persons, Father, Son, and Holy Spirit and yet there is only one God. This great mystery is because of the infinite bond of love that exists between Father, Son, and Holy Spirit. By analogy, there is a profound bond between twins, which unites them together that in its own way becomes a reflection of the nature of God.

ABOUT THE AUTHOR

Msgr. Michael Flannery is a retired Catholic priest of the Diocese of Jackson, Mississippi. He served in diocesan administration for twenty years and in parish ministry for thirty.

After retiring from active ministry five years ago, he took up the art of writing. His first publication is the *Saltillo Mission* that describes the history of a mission in Saltillo, Mexico, which has been jointly sponsored by the Dioceses of Jackson and Biloxi. His second book is the *Prankster Priest* and describes pranks he pulled during his ministry. His third book is *St. Anthony's Eagles* that describes the habits of bald eagles. The eagle is the mascot for a parochial school he was involved in building. His fourth book is *Padre's Christian Stories* and is a collection of short stories. He enjoys writing in his retirement years.

CPSIA information can be obtained
at www.ICGtesting.com
Printed in the USA
BVHW061226030321
601537BV00009B/172